To

_____

_____

From

_____

_____

_____

*To my dear friends Hugh Boyd-Jones and
Morgana Numeriano Lines   C.B.*

Text by Mary Joslin
Illustrations copyright © 2003, 2008, 2013 Christina Balit
This edition copyright © 2013 Lion Hudson

The right of Christina Balit to be identified as the illustrator of this work
has been asserted by her in accordance with the
Copyright, Designs and Patents Act 1988.

Published by Lion Children's Books
an imprint of
Lion Hudson plc
Wilkinson House, Jordan Hill Road,
Oxford OX2 8DR, England
www.lionhudson.com/lionchildrens
ISBN 978 0 7459 6369 3

First edition 2013

A catalogue record for this book is available
from the British Library

Printed and bound in China, December 2012, LH17

The Lion Classic
Wisdom Stories

Retold by MARY JOSLIN
Illustrated by CHRISTINA BALIT

LION
CHILDREN'S

CONTENTS

CONTENTS

CONTENTS

CONTENTS

SPIDER LEARNS A LESSON

A tale from Ghana and the West Indies

LONG AGO THERE lived a spider named Kwaku Anansi. He was very clever and loved nothing more than to outwit others.

"For my next trick," he said to himself, "I shall gather up all the wisdom in the world and keep it for myself. Then I shall be the cleverest creature that can ever be."

He found a pot and he set out to visit all the other creatures in the world.

"I'm collecting wisdom for my pot. Can you let me have some?" he pleaded.

The creatures were generous and Anansi filled his pot to overflowing. "Now I shall tie on the lid so I can keep this wisdom safely hidden," he said to himself.

The only trouble was that the pot was quite large. It was all too easy for anyone to see. What if someone came and stole it?

Anansi began to worry, and then he began to plan.

That night, by starlight, he got up quietly, and secretly took the pot to the base of a tall tree. "Only a spider could get to the top of that," he chuckled. Carefully he began to climb.

Oh dear.

How could he hold the pot and climb? That was a trick he hadn't quite mastered.

He tried holding the pot with his front legs.

Whay oop.

That made him fall over backward. He tried holding it with his back legs. He climbed a little way.

Aarggh.

Then he slid back down. It was time to think again. Hmm.

Luckily he spied a length of silk. It was long and strong and just right for tying the pot to his tummy.

"Now I can climb with all eight legs," he said to himself. And off he went.

Only he couldn't.

Oof.

With the pot in front of him, Anansi could barely touch the trunk with any of his legs. It was so, so annoying.

Just then, his son Ntikuma crept out of the shadows. He had heard his father leaving and had followed to watch what he was up to.

"Try tying it on your back, Dad," he said. "Then it won't be in your way."

Anansi glared at his son. "I'd just thought of that," he lied. "Now scurry off home before you make me angry."

With the pot tied to his back, Anansi set off up the tree. But he was in quite a bad temper and that made him too hasty. Just as he was about to reach the branches, he slipped. And so did the pot.

crack

The pot broke on a rock and all the wisdom spilled out.

crick-crick-CRASH!

All at once lightning flashed and thunder boomed. Rain came down in torrents. As Anansi sheltered in a cluster of leaves, a flood rose. He watched as all the wisdom floated away down to a stream, then on and on and out to sea.

In that way, wisdom spread all around the world, and from that moment on, anyone could find some and make it their own.

"It was a stupid idea to hoard wisdom anyway," grumbled Anansi as he made his way home. "Even when I thought I had it all, a child turned out to have more."

THE EMPEROR'S NEW CLOTHES

Based on a tale by Hans Christian Andersen

THE EMPEROR WAS sitting waiting. He was sitting in his most comfortable chair and wearing his most comfortable afternoon clothes: crimson silk pantaloons and a lovely wrap-style jacket (not unlike a dressing gown but so much more stylish), also in crimson, though a deeper shade, with a contrasting orange border – which was a daring choice – and…

rat tat tat

… not the topic for the afternoon. No. Not after the polite knock on the door. The topic for the afternoon was the following year's parade and here was his chamberlain, eager to present him with the detailed plan of events.

The chamberlain sat down. The chamberlain pulled out his book. The chamberlain began to read. From time to time the chamberlain asked for His Majesty's opinion on the choices that lay before him. His Majesty found it difficult to have an opinion on things to which he had not been paying attention. His Majesty was inclined to accept his chamberlain's recommendations.

"Now we come to the matter of the ceremonial robes," said the chamberlain.

"Robes!" exclaimed the emperor, suddenly interested.

"Historically your forebears have opted for the velvet cape with the…"

"Oh, never mind history!" said the emperor. "Clothes with history are clothes that have been seen before, and what this parade needs is something new, something that looks to the future, something… extraordinary."

The chamberlain slumped a little. Finding new tailors, new designers, new couturiers… he had been doing that for years, and he was running out of options. Did the emperor not understand?

rat tat tat

There was another knock at the door.

"Your Majesty," said a footman. "There are two men at the palace gate who are eager to see you. They say they are the founders of a new and innovative fashion house."

"Aha!" exclaimed the emperor. "Perfect. We were just discussing ceremonial robes. Maybe they will have something of genius to offer."

The chamberlain closed his book and closed his eyes. He waited like that until the two men were brought to the room.

"Your Majesty," said one, bowing low.

"Your Imperial and Royal Majesty," said the other, bending his nose almost to the carpet.

"We bring you a sartorial sensation. The finest fabric the world has yet to see…"

"So fine, so light, so cleverly woven that only the most discerning can appreciate its quality…"

"The foolish, the ignorant – they have neither the eyes to see it nor the wit to care…"

"But you…"

"Your Majesty…"

"Your Imperial and Royal Majesty…"

"You are celebrated beyond this realm as one whose wisdom is unsurpassed."

"So for you we would like to weave the finest robes. You, Your Majesty, are worthy to wear them."

The emperor had listened to their words with growing delight. "This is just what I need," he declared. "I am choosing you to make me robes for next year's parade; robes that will make the crowd say, 'Behold! There is the emperor who will lead us wisely into the future. Hoorah! Hoorah!'"

The two men clapped and bowed and the chamberlain frowned.

"The cost," he said. "What is your charge?"

The two men shuddered as if the thought of talking money was distasteful.

"It will be our pleasure to make these robes as a gift," they said. "All we ask is for the materials, a place to work, and lodgings for while we are here."

And so it was agreed. The men worked in secret, behind locked doors. They lived in the room above the workshops, and the cook brought food to their door. For the work, they asked for silken thread, beads of gold, pearls for buttons…

"I love reading the list of supplies," the emperor told his chamberlain. "I can only dream of what they're making."

The making went on for weeks. More materials were asked for. More materials were supplied. The chamberlain was a tiny bit worried that all anyone could do was dream of what they making. What was happening with all those costly materials?

"We have everything in hand," was all the answer he got. The weavers murmured about the importance of keeping "The Robes" top secret. The day of the parade was getting near. The men came and measured the emperor. It was time to cut into the amazing fabric and begin to stitch. They needed just a few more things to finish off a perfect job.

"I hope you're going to be ready on time," grumbled the chamberlain. "Everything is ready for the parade except these fancy robes. Unless I see some progress, I'm going to have to bring out the treasured historical velvet cape…"

"All will be done," said the men. "The day before – the morning of the day before, in fact, so as not to leave you fretting — we will come and let the emperor try on his new clothes."

True to their word, they arrived on the appointed day with a wheeled wardrobe. They unlocked it. They whispered to one another. One opened the door with a flourish.

"May the wise see and admire!" declared the other.

The emperor was silent. Was it awe? Was it wonder? What would he say?

"Oh my!" said the emperor. His voice sounded a little squeaky. "I'm overawed. The robes are... indescribable... and the colour... it's beyond words... What would you call it, Chamberlain?"

In truth, the emperor could see nothing in the wardrobe. Nor could his chamberlain. But what was the latter to do? Reveal himself to be a fool? One who didn't have the eyes to see nor the wit to care? That would never do. He must think... and quickly.

"The purple dye we supplied — it was very expensive, but worth it for what you've done with it. Wonderful. With the gold. And the pearl buttons. And everything. I'm not really a clothes expert like His Majesty, though."

"His Imperial and Royal Majesty," corrected the two men. "Tomorrow, his Imperial and Royal Majesty will wear these astonishing robes for the great parade."

The king nodded a little frantically. "You must make a proclamation," he told his chamberlain, "to ensure that the populace is prepared for the magnificence they are to behold. I'm sure there are more than a few who will need to be educated to appreciate the robes fully."

The chamberlain hurried to issue an announcement. He told the courtiers, he told the coachman, he told the heralds, he told the town crier… He even went to the marketplace and mingled with the crowds to make sure everyone knew to cheer loudly when they saw the emperor in his amazing clothes.

The next day the two men came to array the emperor in the fine clothes.

"The shirt," said the men. "Then the breeches. And the cloak. And the sash. And the turban. We are honoured that you accept our work. And now, you go your way, and we go ours. It has been our honour and reward to serve you."

The emperor nodded. He tried not to shiver as he climbed into the open carriage. *He couldn't even feel the clothes. They were surely wonderful, but not windproof.* He steadied himself as the coachmen drove it toward the gate. He entered the square.

"Hoorah! Hoorah!" The noise from the crowd came like a wave. It rose, it grew, it reached a crescendo and then… quiet. Was it awe? Was it wonder?

From his father's shoulders a little boy spoke, his voice as clear as a bell.

"Why has that man got no clothes on?"

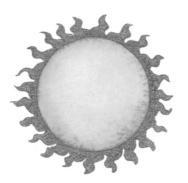

THE THREE WANDERERS

A tale from the Bura tribe in Nigeria

No one knew where the three wanderers had come from, and no one knew where they were going.

"Clearly one is wealthy," whispered the villagers. "Look at his bangles, his earrings, and his necklaces. And what can it be that he carries in that cloth bundle?"

"And the second is prosperous," they agreed. "You can tell from the size of his belly that he eats more than the other two. And what can it be that he carries in that basket?"

Then their attention turned to the third. He was thin and his clothing was the most simple. He did not appear to be carrying anything with him.

"At least he has the advantage of travelling light," was the best

they could agree on. "While the others huff and puff and shift their load from arm to arm, he has breath enough to sing."

The wanderers walked on. They came to a man who was sitting in the shade of a tree. "We are looking for a place to stay," said the three wanderers. "Are you able to offer us hospitality?"

The man looked at them and pointed to the one who wore the most jewels. "I would welcome one of you," he said, "but I am a poor man. The other two must ask elsewhere."

The three wanderers exchanged glances. "I am sorry," said the one who had been chosen. "I fear that if I stayed with you, my small supply of wealth would soon be gone. We must travel on together."

Some time later they came to another man, who was sitting by a well. "We are looking for a place to stay," said the three wanderers. "Are you able to offer us hospitality?"

The man looked at them and pointed to the one who had the roundest belly. "I would welcome one of you," he said, "but I am a hungry man with little food to offer. The other two must ask elsewhere."

The three wanderers exchanged glances. "I am sorry," said the one who had been chosen. "I fear that if I stayed with you, my small supply of food would soon be gone. We must travel on together."

It was many miles before they saw a man gathering wild berries to eat. He waved at the three wanderers and came to greet them.

"We are looking for a place to stay," said the three wanderers. "Are you able to offer us hospitality?"

"I live very simply," replied the man. "I recognize the one among you who might be happy to stay with me. I fear that I could not provide for you, sir, who appear to be wealthy, nor you, sir, who appear to have plenty to eat."

The men clapped their hands and laughed. "Let us all come and stay with you," they said, "for you have chosen to welcome the wise man. Wisdom is never used up, but brings wealth and plenty with it."

THE STORY THAT GREW

Based on a tale from Bengal

IT WAS LATE in the afternoon, the time when the light of the western sun turns all the world to gold. A farmer was walking home from the fields, glad that the day's hard work was done. He was singing loudly and cheerfully his usual plodding-along song when…

whrrrr

All of a sudden, just a step away, a lark flew up into the air, trilling its thrilling song high up into the sky.

The man watched open-mouthed as the bird vanished into the blue.

As he walked on and began his next song, he felt something in his mouth.

Bleh.

He pulled it out.

It was a feather.

"How curious," he said. "That's never happened before."

When he reached home, he recounted the incident to his wife.

"It must have been a feather from the lark you saw," she said, laughing.

"Of course!" agreed the man. "I wish I could sing like a lark."

The following day, the woman went down to the well as usual to fetch water. It was a time to swap stories and to laugh together.

"A funny thing happened to my husband," the wife told a neighbour. "He was walking along, singing, when a lark feather flew out of his mouth."

"How curious," said the neighbour. "I've never heard of such a thing."

As she walked home, the neighbour met her sister and they stopped to exchange their news.

"Never say that nothing interesting happens around here," she announced. "I've just heard the most astonishing thing from the farmer's wife. Her husband was out in the fields the other day when a lark flew out of his mouth and began to sing. Imagine that: it was as if he'd been given the gift of song in the form of a bird."

"Well, I never," agreed the sister. She continued on her way to the market in the nearby town and began to make her usual purchases.

"I don't suppose there's much news from your quiet little village, is there?" said the stallholder.

"Indeed, there is," said the sister. "A local farmer has suddenly been given the most wonderful talent for singing. When he opens his mouth, larks fly out and soar up into the blue."

"My goodness!" replied the stallholder. "That is quite sensational. Thank you for letting me know before this marvel is the talk of the town."

As the stallholder chatted to her customers that day, the marvel did become the talk of the town.

"Have you spoken to the stallholder today?" the people said to one another. "You know she's friends with a woman from the next-door village. Well, the friend's sister's neighbour's husband has been given the gift of song…"

"And when he sings, larks fly out of his mouth."

"Larks and warblers."

"Larks and warblers *and* songthrushes."

"*And* cuckoos."

"*And* a pair of golden orioles."

"*And then* swifts and swallows come dipping and diving overhead."

"*And then* all the world turns to gold."

The women of the town were very excited that such an amazing thing had happened in such an ordinary place as where they lived.

"We must go and see for ourselves," they agreed. They arranged

for a man who owned a donkey cart to take them all at once to the village to hear the farmer and see the wonder.

When they reached the village, the sun was dipping low in the sky and the farmer was just coming up the road.

"Please," the women begged him. "Sing for us."

"Oh, all right," said the man. And he began to sing loudly and cheerfully his usual plodding-along song.

The women listened politely to the end of the verse.

"What about the birds?" they said. "When do the birds come and lift the melody?"

"Birds?" said the farmer. "What birds?"

Waiting for a Rabbit

A tale from China

THE FARMER HAD spent the morning planting rice seedlings in his paddy field.

"How my back aches," he complained to himself. "If I wear myself out, I won't be able to finish the planting."

He left the paddy field and found a little spot in the shade of a tree. There he sat and dozed a little as the heat rose with the sun.

Suddenly...

THUMP

Something hit the tree. The slender trunk shook and a few leaves fluttered to the ground.

The farmer shook himself awake and looked around. There

was a rabbit lying dead on the ground. He looked up. The fox that must have been chasing the rabbit was trotting away, its tail almost invisible in the long grass.

"A rabbit," said the farmer, lifting the lifeless body. "What a treat." He took the rabbit home and prepared it for his supper. Then he cleaned the skin and took it to the market, where he sold it for a good price.

"This is the way to make a living," he said to himself. "All I have to do is sit under the tree and wait for the next rabbit to come along."

The next day he sat in the shade, watching his neighbours planting their fields. "They do look weary," he said to himself, and he felt rather pleased with how he had decided to spend the day.

zzzzz

He dozed and he watched and he watched and he dozed. No rabbit came crashing into the tree. The farmer started doing sums in his head… "Even if I only get a rabbit every other day, I will still make a better living than my neighbours," he decided. "So I shall wait here tomorrow."

The next day came and went. No rabbit came crashing into the tree.

Yet more days went by. The farmer's neighbours had planted their paddy fields and the young plants were growing strongly. The fox trotted by from time to time, but still no rabbits came anywhere near the tree.

The farmer's paddy field turned green with weeds. "You must not wait any longer," his neighbours warned him. "You cannot count on rabbits crashing into trees in order to make your living."

Glumly the farmer set to work. But by the time he had cleared his paddy field of weeds, he had undone the planting of that first morning, and he was late planting fresh seedlings. They did not grow well and so he had a very poor crop to harvest.

Dazzled by Dreams

An Iroquois legend

THERE WAS ONCE a girl who was dazzled by dreams. "I am growing up now," she told her mother, "and there is so much I dream of doing.

"I want to marry a handsome man, and I want him to be a brave and strong hunter who will be able to bring me all I need."

"Daydreams won't bring you food or fuel," answered her mother. "Even so, your father and I have been thinking that it is time for you to be getting married. I shall make arrangements for the young sons of our clan to come and meet you."

One by one they came, but the girl was not impressed.

"That last one was too shabby," she complained. "Did you see his moccasins?

"And the one before stumbled so much in his speaking I could barely find out anything about him.

"And the one before that was too short and rather flabby.

"They certainly won't give me the life I dream of. I shall go on looking."

One night, when the girl was sitting with her family around the cooking fire, a stranger came to the door: a warrior who looked both young and strong.

"Come in!" said the mother; but the warrior stayed outside and pointed at the girl.

"The people of my clan have heard that you are a powerful dreamer," he said. "I have come to ask you to be my wife."

The girl could hardly believe it. Hers were no idle dreams, then; rather a foretelling of the future. And her special talent had been noticed by someone quite dazzling. The warrior was tall and handsome, and his movements strong and graceful. Around his waist he wore a belt of black and yellow wampum, and on his head two tall feathers.

"Mother, I must get my things ready and go!" she declared.

The mother was worried. "There are still plenty of young men for you to meet who belong to our clan," she said. "It is dangerous to go with a stranger. You do not know his people nor their customs."

But the girl was determined to follow her dreams. She gathered her belongings and followed the stranger into the starlit night. The moon sailed across its heavenly ocean. On earth, the fireflies danced.

As they walked, a breeze began to blow. Clouds rolled in across the sky. The path plunged into a shadowy wood.

"Is it far?" she whispered to the warrior. "I do not know this trail."

"We are nearly there," said the warrior. Together they slithered down a steep bank alongside a waterfall and in a little while came to a lodge. The antlers of a giant elk were fastened above the door. There was a smell of... was it fish? Well, they were near the river.

Through the remainder of the night the girl sat alone in a corner of the lodge, huddled in her own blanket. In the morning the warrior returned, carrying a dress decorated with wampum.

"Put this on," he said. "It will be a sign that you are willing to join our clan. Then you will be ready to meet my people. I will return shortly."

The girl looked at the dress. Somehow the wampum reminded her of scales. It smelled of... was it fish? She looked out at the morning mist. The world was grey.

As she was wondering what to do, a serpent came slithering through the door and stared. She gasped in fear and sat transfixed. Then she noted the glittering bands of gold and black.

They had the same pattern as the warrior's wampum belt.

The girl rushed outside. As she did so, what seemed like hundreds of serpents slithered into hiding. Were these the

warrior's people? And what would she become if she put on the wampum dress?

She closed her eyes and wished for help. At once, she seemed to see the face of an old man.

"Granddaughter," he said, "you must leave this place and not turn back. You will come to a steep cliff, and you must climb it bravely. Do not be tempted to give up. Do not be dazzled if the sun shines in your eyes. Do not give in to wild imaginings."

The girl opened her eyes and looked. There was the warrior, strong and handsome. He was smiling and reaching out his hand.

As quick as a bird, she fled. She heard the warrior shout her name, but she did not answer. She hurt her fingers clambering up the cliff, but she did not flinch at the pain. As a fierce sun broke through the clouds, she closed her eyes. But she could not close her ears.

All around there came hissing and spitting. Had the serpents followed her? And what had touched her leg? Were they twining around her, conspiring to pull her down?

All at once, thunder rolled like drums of war. Lightning flashed like spears across the sky. The girl reached the top of the cliff and glanced fearfully behind her. The thunderbolts were striking the serpents, and they hissed and twisted before vanishing into nothing.

When at last the thunder and lightning stopped, the sky cleared to a bright blue. The girl again heard the voice of the old man.

"Thank you, Granddaughter. You have helped me rid the earth of those evil creatures. Your brave deed has awakened a great power within you. One day, I may need to call upon you to use it again to defeat the power of evil. For now, go back to your people, and be content with simple things."

The girl went on her way, dazzled no longer by her dreams but by the glittering archway of a rainbow above her home.

THE WISE MAN AND THE PUMPKIN

A tale from Turkey

THE WISE MAN was sitting under a walnut tree. It was early
afternoon; although the sun was hot, the walnut tree leaves
gave good shade.

Of course, a wise man does not cease from deep reflection,
even in the hours of rest, and it gave him pleasure to sit and
reflect on the wisdom of the world's great Maker.

"Such a lovely tree the Maker has created," he said to himself.
"Its broad leaves, its green shade, and of course, the many
delicious nuts dangling from the boughs. They are a treat from
harvest time all through the hungry winter months."

He looked out into the shimmering heat of the afternoon. There was a vegetable garden.

"The pumpkins are ripening nicely," he said to himself. "The sun and the rain have enabled them to grow to a magnificent size. They too will provide through the winter. How generous is the world's great Maker."

He pondered some more. "It's odd, though, isn't it," he thought, "to create such a mighty tree with such famously strong wood for such tiny walnuts? Meanwhile, those giant pumpkins grow on a vine so weak it can only crawl along the ground."

Thinking this – and in spite of his love of thinking – he dozed off.

The afternoon wore on. As the sun sank lower, the shadows grew longer. A cool breeze fluttered the leaves of the walnut tree.

A walnut fell. By chance, it hit the wise man right on the nose.

Ouch.

He woke up in consternation and rubbed the sore spot.

Then he spied the fallen nut. He looked up at the tree. He looked out at the vegetable patch.

"Oh dear," he exclaimed. "If pumpkins grew on that tree, I would have been badly hurt. How wise is the world's great Maker."

THE WOODCUTTER OF GURA

A tale from Ethiopia

THE WOODCUTTER MOPPED his brow and sighed. How many miles had he trudged from his home in Gura? And how far must he trudge along this dried-up riverbed to find a tree worth bothering with? It was such a chore getting enough firewood.

As he rounded a jumble of rocks, his eyes lit up. There was a large, dead olive tree. It would fuel fires in his house for many weeks, and it was his for the taking.

He scrambled up into its branches and seated himself on the sturdiest branch. Then he began to chop.

swing... chop

swing... chop

swing... chop

An elder from a nearby village happened to come past. He looked up and wagged his finger.

"What are you trying to do up there?" he called.

"I'm chopping this tree for firewood," the woodcutter replied.

swing... chop

"That's no way to go about it!" cried the elder.

"Yes it is," answered the woodcutter.

swing... chop

"You should cut the tree down first and then lop the branches off," insisted the elder. "If you go on chopping the branch you're sitting on, you'll fall and kill yourself."

The man glared down. "I'm a woodcutter and chopping is what I do," he replied.

"Don't blame me when you're dead," said the elder. And he walked off.

swing... chop

swing... chop

swing... CRAASH

All at once, the branch on which the woodcutter had been sitting gave way. He fell to the ground in a tangle of twigs and lay there, stunned.

"Oh my," he said to himself. "I've gone and killed myself. I should have listened to the elder. I'm dead, and there's no one to blame but myself."

He closed his eyes and let his mind go blank.

After a while some friends from Gura came along. They were distressed to see that the woodcutter had clearly fallen from the tree and they hurried to revive him.

"Can you hear us? Wake up! Say something! Please!"

The woodcutter lay still and limp. He'd killed himself. He'd never be able to talk to his friends again.

"He's dead," the friends agreed. "We should at least carry him back to his wife and arrange his funeral."

They used one of their cloaks to make a stretcher, laid the woodcutter on it carefully, and set off.

"Don't forget the axe," murmured the woodcutter.

Without really thinking, one of the men darted back to fetch the axe and laid it next to the man.

Not long after, they came to a point where a trail led away from the deep gravel of the riverbed.

"That's the best way back," said one.

"The trail is shorter, but it goes over the hill," replied another. "So it will be much harder to carry our load."

And they began to argue among themselves which way to choose.

"I always used to choose the trail," said the woodcutter.

Without really thinking, the men set off along the trail.

"It's what our friend would have wanted," they agreed.

Their arrival at the village caused a commotion. The elders who had gathered in the shade hurried over, demanding to know what had happened.

"We found the woodcutter lying on the ground under an olive tree," they explained. "A branch fell off without warning and killed him."

The woodcutter on his stretcher shook his head weakly. "That's not how it was," he protested. "I was sitting on the branch that I was chopping. I only have myself to blame for being dead."

The elders didn't seem to notice who had spoken. They had begun to argue about who should tell his wife and what they should do for the funeral. The woodcutter on his stretcher was left on the ground.

As the friends debated with the elders, a dog came along and licked the woodcutter's face.

"Get rid of that mutt!" exclaimed the woodcutter. "Is there no respect for the dead any more?"

The friends chased the dog away and the elders agreed that the man must be carried at once into the shade. "We can at least be a little cooler while we think about what to do," they agreed.

The woodcutter pushed himself up on his elbows. "Send for my wife! She's probably down by the well with the other women doing the washing."

"Good idea!" agreed the men, and someone hurried to fetch the woodcutter's wife. Within a few minutes she came running, screaming in grief, while behind her the village women wailed and wept.

An elder stepped forward to offer his support. "An olive branch fell on him and killed him," he explained as gently as he could.

The man sat up. "I told you before. I was sitting on the branch I was chopping. An elder from along the road came and warned me. He said I'd kill myself. And he was right." He sank back onto the stretcher.

"Ah, yes," sighed one of the friends. "He did tell us. He fell from the tree and killed himself."

The woodcutter's wife put her hands on her hips. "But if he can talk, what makes you think he's dead?"

"We found him dead," said the friends.

"And now he's told us how he died," agreed the elders.

"But he's talking," said the wife. Around her, the village women fell silent.

The woodcutter sat up and put his hands on his hips. "Listen everyone," he said. "The elder from the next village said I'd kill myself, then he turned and went. He is the wisest man for miles. He only ever speaks the truth. If he said I'd kill myself, I'm dead."

"But perhaps he was warning you," said his wife. "Did he see you fall?"

"Oh, will no one believe me?" said the woodcutter. "I'm not putting up with all this nonsense."

He stood up, grabbed his axe, and set off down the trail.

"Where are you going?" cried the villagers.

"To chop some wood!" he replied.

SILVER ON THE HEARTH

A tale from Afghanistan

THE FARMER AND his wife were very poor. They worked hard enough, toiling in the fields through all the daylight hours; even so, their land produced barely enough crops to feed them. It was rare that they had any surplus to sell.

Late one afternoon, when the man was weeding in his field, he caught the sleeve of his coat on a bramble. It tore the cloth and scratched the man's arm so it bled.

"Vicious plant! I'm getting rid of you," he declared, and he set to work digging out the bramble.

As he dug, his spade struck against a stone. He scrabbled in the earth to lift it clear… and when he did so, he saw a dirty knotted cloth underneath.

He pulled away the bramble and began to dig more deeply to find out what was there. He pulled out the bundle, untied the knots… and there was a pottery jar. When he lifted the lid, he saw a hoard of silver coins.

"Oh my!" he said to himself. "So much money… this would set me free from so many worries."

He was thinking how best to carry it home when another thought struck him.

"The money isn't mine. Though it is my field. But to whom should I take it? I shall have to think about what is the right thing to do."

Hurriedly he put the pot back in the hole and flung the bramble over it.

That evening he told his wife about the find.

She was really angry. "You just left good money in your own field!" she cried. "I can't think of anyone who could have buried it, and I can't think of anyone who needs it more than we do."

The man argued that he wanted to be sure that it was his to spend, but his wife kept on shouting.

A neighbour passing by the house heard what she said, and he stopped to listen.

Very interesting.

That night, by moonlight, he went to the field and easily found the newly dug hole. He took the jar and raced home.

"Now let's find out what's inside," he said as he lifted the lid.

To his dismay, a poisonous snake darted out its head and hissed. The neighbour clamped the lid on the jar and slumped into a chair.

"My neighbour... he's trying to kill me!" he whispered.

"The screaming and shouting… it was a trap. Well, I'll make him the victim of his own wicked plan."

He fetched a ladder and crept around to the farmer's house. Then he climbed up on to the chimney and threw the contents of the jar down to the hearth. Below, the fire had been dampened down for the night, but the tumbling coins sent orange embers flying.

In the morning, the farmer awoke and was dismayed to see the mess where the fire should have been.

Then he looked more closely.

All he could find among the ruins of the fire was a dead snake… and a pile of silver coins.

"Look at this!" he called to his wife. "All this money – it must be meant for us. Whatever the rights and wrongs of the treasure I found, this must surely be a gift."

THE BOASTFUL TURTLE

A tale from India

A TURTLE WAS SITTING on a rock by the edge of the river, enjoying the warmth of the sun. The sound of voices disturbed his dreaming.

"I'm seeing plenty of turtles along the riverbank," said one of the speakers. "Let's come back with nets and catch a few. They are good eating."

"That's an excellent idea," agreed more voices. "We'll come straight back."

splish

The turtle plopped into the water. The men wanted to eat him. He must think of a way to escape – and fast.

Then he had an idea. A clever idea. An amazingly clever idea.

He felt extremely proud of himself. So he swam out into the river to talk to two cranes who were fishing with their long beaks.

"I need to find a way to escape the hunters," he explained, waving his flippers excitedly. "If you two hold a long stick between your beaks, you could fly together with it, couldn't you?"

The cranes thought for a moment before nodding their heads.

"And if I closed my mouth around the middle of the stick, then you could carry me far away from those hunters."

"You could indeed," agreed the cranes. "You'll have to hold on tight, of course."

The men were returning with their nets when the two cranes flew up into the air, carrying the turtle on the stick.

"My goodness," they exclaimed. "Those clever birds have found a way to carry a turtle."

The turtle was annoyed. "It was my idea!" he called.

The Ant and the Grain
of Wheat

A tale from Italy

A GOLDEN SUN WAS setting over a golden field.

"It's been a good year," agreed the harvesters. "Our wheat has grown tall and the ears are full of grain.

"Now we can load up the sheaves and take them for threshing. We shall have plenty to eat when the winter brings cold weather to the empty fields."

In the days that followed, the ants came to forage among the stubble. They scurried to gather up any fallen grains and carry them back to the anthill, undaunted that each grain was larger than themselves.

For several days they gathered the food they would need for winter. Fallen grains became harder and harder to find. Still the ants were eager to fill their stores.

march and march and march and march

The need to keep on marching was the only thing the little ant knew about. He was carrying one last grain, and it was very heavy.

As he reached the edge of the field, the grain of wheat suddenly spoke. "Why not leave me here?" it asked.

The ant let the grain fall.

"Thank you," said the grain. "Please don't take me into your store. I'm not just food. I'm a seed. I dream of sleeping through the winter in the good brown soil. Then, in the spring, I will grow into a plant. In the summer I will grow tall. When at last I produce an ear full of plump grain, it will be harvest time, and you can gather it up for next year's store."

The ant thought. "I've been told we need everything in the anthill," it replied.

53

"If you use up all the seeds this year, how will you have any next year?" asked the grain.

The ant was puzzled. "You mean, if I push you into a little hole like this...

"and then..."

oof

"push earth on top like this...

"you will grow."

"Yes," called the grain somewhat faintly. The ant watched and waited.

"I can't see you growing."

"Come back next harvest time," said the grain. "Now if you don't mind, I'm feeling sleepy."

To be honest, the ant did not think much about the one grain of wheat. It was not until the following year when it came marching –

march and march and march and march

– to forage for grains that it remembered.

There was its seed, now tall and golden and bearing a full ear of grain.

Beyond, the harvesters were once again at work in the field they themselves had sown.

Poor Little Rich Girl

A tale from Poland

ZUZIA WAS A merchant's daughter, and she was both rich and pretty.

From the time she was a baby, servants had looked after her and they had always told her that she was adorable. Zuzia grew up thinking she deserved always to have her own way.

But although the servants doted on Zuzia, the girls of her own age found her ill-tempered. Zuzia began to notice that when the other girls danced together, she was left on her own.

"What is the matter with them all?" she complained to her old nurse. "I want to snap my fingers and make them like me at once."

"Oh, if you want a change like that, then you had better go and see the wise woman who lives on the mountain," advised the grey-haired servant.

"I shall send one of the stable lads with a message," replied Zuzia. "I am sure that the old crone will tell me how to get what I want for a bag of coins."

The messenger went, but returned at sunset with the bag of coins still full.

"The wise woman said that if you want to know how to make people invite you to join in their dancing, then you must go to her yourself," he explained. "And she said that you must go on foot."

Zuzia frowned and pouted, and for a week she refused to go.

Then she began to see that while she did nothing, there would be no change.

"I suppose I shall have to go myself," she sulked, and she ordered the servants to prepare what she needed for the journey: smart little boots of the finest leather, a warm woollen cloak, and a bag of food.

She set off in the early morning through the streets of the town and on to the track that led into the hills.

As she walked, she began to feel her smart boots pinching her toes. She was glad when she saw a cottage where an old woman was sitting on a bench by the front door.

"Oh, my feet are hurting so badly," Zuzia exclaimed, sitting down beside her. "Yet I have to walk all the way to the wise woman who lives on the mountain."

The old woman looked at Zuzia. She looked at the fine boots and then she took off her own shoes.

"These battered things are my only pair," said the woman, "but they have stretched so much over the years that they have grown too big for me. They might fit you better than what you have on."

Zuzia was in too much pain to care about how misshapen the shoes looked. She was delighted at how comfortable they felt. She gave her boots to the woman and walked on.

As Zuzia climbed higher toward the mountain, the air grew cold and the wind began to blow her cloak around. Then grey clouds gathered and rain began to fall in great, heavy drops.

Zuzia was glad to find a woodsman's cottage among the trees.

"Thank goodness," she cried, running under the porch where the woodsman stood. "I would be wet through with just this woollen cloak."

The woodsman looked her up and down. "You'd be better off with the canvas tarpaulin I have on the bed. But my wife is sick and we need to use it to help keep her warm."

"Might you exchange it for my cloak?" asked Zuzia politely.

"If you wish," agreed the woodsman. He brought a ragged

square of canvas for Zuzia to wrap around her shoulders, and he took her cloak respectfully.

Zuzia trudged on, hour after hour, nibbling from her bag of food as she went.

As she reached the higher slopes, she came to a shepherd's cottage. Somewhere a child was crying.

The mother came out to see who was passing and comforted the child. "He's just very hungry," she explained. "My husband has taken sheep to market and will be back with supplies, but that's tomorrow at the earliest."

Zuzia opened her bag. "I've already eaten today," she said, "and I've got a lot of bread and cheese left."

She handed the bag to the mother, and the little boy gave her a hug.

She hugged him back, then hurried on up the mountain, eager now to find the wise woman before nightfall. Wearily she knocked on the door of the little hut. There was no answer. Zuzia knocked again. Still no one came.

"I have come so far – and all for nothing!" Zuzia complained. Then, suddenly anxious, she tried turning the door handle to the hut. Finding it open, she went inside to shelter for the night.

To her surprise, she found that the bed was spread with freshly cut herbs and flowers, and lying among them was a message.

"I have been expecting you, but I had to go elsewhere. Stay here for one night. When you go back, you will have what you wished for."

Too tired to care, Zuzia lay down and slept. The following morning she set off as the sun rose.

When she reached the shepherd's hut, she found the mother and the son mending buckets and laughing. "We shall get a lot done today," she said. "We both feel much better for a good meal."

Zuzia was surprised to realize that she still didn't feel hungry.

When she reached the woodsman's cottage, she saw the wife sitting wrapped in the woollen cloak, enjoying the sunshine.

"I slept so well for being warm, I've been able to get up at last," she explained.

Zuzia realized that the canvas square had served her very well through the rain and refused to accept the cloak.

When she reached the old woman's house, she found the woman ironing.

"I'm just getting ready to go to my niece's wedding tomorrow," she said. "I was hoping I might be able to keep your lovely boots a little longer, for they are so much smarter than my shoes, and they fit me well."

"Oh, keep them for ever," replied Zuzia. "The ones you gave me have been the most comfortable I've ever worn."

"They were good shoes once," said the woman. "I bought them for going to a dance. They were lovely then… and they've lasted. Perhaps you'll enjoy dancing in them again."

Zuzia's face lit up. "I'll try," she said.

And with that, she danced all the way to town.

A group of girls she knew saw her skipping and twirling. She smiled at them and clapped her hands.

"That looks fun!" they called. "Can you teach us how to dance with you?"

THE EAGLE AND THE
JACKDAW

Based on a tale by Aesop, from ancient Greece

FROM ITS PERCH on a high crag, the eagle watched. Its eyes picked out every movement in the meadow below: the mouse shuffling through the rough grass; a pair of songbirds darting among the seed heads… and the huddle of sheep seeking out the last of the grazing among the tumble of boulders.

The eagle spread its wings and soared upward. This was the time to be patient: to drift high above the mountain, watching as the smallest of the sheep – one of this year's lambs – began to follow the line of green grass along a trickle of water. Soon it would be some distance away from its mother.

Now.

The eagle swooped down on the unsuspecting lamb and grabbed it with its talons. The lamb bleated and struggled, but it was no use. The eagle flapped its wings and carried it as if it were no more than a bundle of rags high, high, high… up to the eyrie where its own chicks were waiting to be fed.

From its own vantage point, a jackdaw watched and cackled. What a trick that eagle had played! Yet it had taken a lamb – a mere bundle of bones compared with the ram that was even now clambering out of the dry riverbed.

The jackdaw flapped. He soared, he swooped… he sank his claws into the ram's thick fleece.

He flapped and flapped, but he could not lift that ram. Worse than that, he could not disentangle his claws. And here came the shepherd, shouting and waving his stick.

"You thieving bird," he cried as he smothered the jackdaw in a piece of old sacking. "Did you think you could have one of my sheep like that eagle? Well, I'm going to have you as a pet for my boy instead. "

He took the jackdaw back home and clipped its feathers.

The shepherd's young son came running to see. "What have you brought, Dad?"

"It's a jackdaw," said the shepherd, "but I caught him trying to fly off with a ram.

"He thinks he's an eagle. Silly bird."

TRUST THE DONKEY

A Sioux legend

THE YOUNG BRIDE was not only beautiful – she was also the daughter of a powerful chief. The warrior who was to be her husband knew that their children would be part of a great and highly respected family.

After they were married, the young woman gave birth to twins. The chief was delighted, and he came with rich gifts for his little grandsons. Then he invited all the people who loved and respected him to a great celebration.

The grandmother of the infant boys came with a special gift of her own. "I have made two saddlebags in which the youngsters can travel," she said. "Here too is a donkey. He is patient and wise and will carry them safely."

Some months later, the warrior decided to take his family on
a hunting journey.

"I have a fine pony who will carry my sons," he told his wife.
"The donkey is better suited to carrying the baggage."

The wife loaded the donkey in the traditional manner. She
lashed the long tipi poles in two bundles and tied them on either
side of the donkey's back so they trailed on the ground behind
the animal. Then she tied in cross poles to make a travois — a

sledge onto which she could pile all the cooking pots, the sleeping mats, and the skin tent itself.

She had just finished when her husband put the saddlebags on the pony and carefully lifted his sons into them. The donkey began to stamp and to kick. He grew so wild that other villagers hurried to control him before he damaged the travois and everything on it.

The grandmother came hurrying too, and she soothed the braying donkey while everything was unloaded.

"I told you the donkey was to carry the saddlebags and my little grandsons," she admonished. "He knows how precious they are. It was an insult to him to load him up with all the baggage."

When the two little boys were loaded onto the donkey's back, he became perfectly quiet and obedient. The hunting party set out.

They had only been gone a day when they were ambushed. A band of enemies came riding furiously on their ponies, some firing arrows and others brandishing sticks.

The warrior and his fighting men rode to meet them, whooping their terrifying war cry. Birds rose up in terror from the bushes and sped away, shrieking in alarm. There followed violence and bloodshed. Terrible deeds were done by warriors on both sides before the battle was over.

The wife went to tend her husband, who was wounded and weary.

"My sons," he said. "Were you able to keep my sons safe?"

To the wife's horror, she could not find them. "I led them to safety," she said, "but then I turned to watch and then I had to run and…"

She began to shriek and sob.

"I have won a battle and lost my sons," wept the warrior.

The husband and wife clung together and wept as the other hunters gathered up their possessions. Then everyone trooped back to the village.

Outside her tipi, the grandmother was patting the donkey.

"I said you should trust the donkey," she said. "He arrived some time ago and brought your sons safely home."

Under the Banyan Tree

A tale from Bhutan

BELOW THE HUGE and ancient Himalayan mountains, the slopes are covered in forest. There, somewhere, in a clearing long ago, stood a banyan tree. Four creatures used to meet around its trunk: an elephant, a monkey, a rabbit, and a quail. They would talk about everything under the sun.

The problem was that they could not always agree among themselves, and sometimes their conversations turned to quarrelling. Whose opinion should they trust the most? How could they decide?

"Well, I'm certainly bigger than all of you," said the elephant, "so I think my view should have the most weight."

"Knowing what is right has nothing to do with size," protested

the monkey. "It has to do with wisdom, and wisdom comes with experience, and experience comes with age."

"I have seen many seasons," declared the elephant. "I have rested in the shade of this banyan tree since I was a child, and see how far its branches now spread."

"I have been coming to this banyan tree for longer," argued the monkey. "I have been feasting on its figs year after year. I was among its branches when you first came and rubbed yourself against its trunk. That means I am older, and therefore what I say is more to be trusted."

The rabbit sat on its hind legs and fidgeted with its whiskers.

"I totally agree with Monkey," he said to the elephant, "insofar as it is age that brings wisdom. But if I may be so bold, I have made my home around this banyan tree for longer

than either of you. I nibbled its leaves when it was such a small plant that I could actually reach the young growth. That means I have known this banyan tree for more seasons than Monkey,

and therefore I am wiser than either of you."

All this time, the quail had been sitting listening, cocking its head this way and that as each of the creatures spoke. Now it flapped its wings and spoke.

"When I was young, I grew up in the

shade of another banyan tree. I pecked some of its fallen fruit on the day I scampered away from my nest to find my own home. It was here that I laid my droppings, and from the seed within them, this tree has grown."

The quail nodded its head as if agreeing with itself and gave a little cluck.

"Eeek," said the rabbit.

"Oohooh," said the monkey.

"Aha," said the elephant.

"You are the oldest," they agreed. "We must respect your opinion before our own."

And with the matter settled, the four creatures lived as friends under the shade of the banyan tree.

A Bowl of Milk

A Parsi tale, from Persia and India

PRINCE JADI RANA had returned from a tour of the country he ruled. He was pleased with what he had seen.

"My people are not wealthy," he said, "but they have enough. Those that farm the soil can grow fruit and field crops; down by the shore, fishermen harvest the sea.

"I consider it my duty to enable them to live peaceable and honest lives."

But a land to call home can be hard to find, and for this reason, the calm of the prince's reign was soon to be challenged.

"Tumultuous news," said his messenger. "People have come from over the sea seeking a homeland. They are landing at Sanjan, and there are very many of them. They wear outlandish

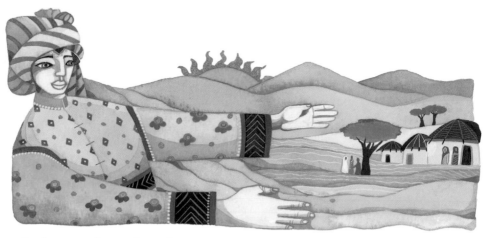

clothes, and we fear the men have swords concealed about their person."

"Who are these foreigners?" Jadi Rana demanded to know. "How dare they disturb my people and threaten their wellbeing?"

He did not have to wait long to find out. Another messenger arrived – one of the foreigners, who bowed low before he made his request.

"We have had to flee our ancient homeland," he explained. "A warlike people came and conquered us. They demanded that we follow their ways and their beliefs – that we become like them and cease to be ourselves. We seek a place where we can be free to live as we believe is right."

Jadi Rana listened as the foreigner made his plea. The messenger spoke haltingly and with many mistakes; however, the prince himself did not speak any of the foreigners' language. He wanted to explain that though he did not want to be cruel, his duty and his loyalty were to his own people. After some time spent in thought, he whispered to a servant, who returned with a bowl full of milk.

"Take this to the leader of your people," he told the foreigner. "It is the best answer I can give."

Down by the shore, the foreigners waited to hear what news the messenger might bring. Could they stay? Must they go? Would they have to defend themselves in battle?

The messenger carried the bowl of milk up to their leader, who was old enough to have faced many problems and wise enough to have solved them.

He saw the bowl of milk, filled to the brim, and he understood what Prince Jadi Rana was trying to say. Smiling, he asked for some sugar and added a pinch of it to the bowl of milk.

"Take that to the prince and ask him to taste it," he said.

Jadi Rana understood at once. "The people may stay," he announced, "and they must be free to follow their own customs.

"However, they must learn our language, they must wear our style of clothing, and they must give up their weapons.

"Then they will live among us as sugar in milk: all mixed in and making life sweeter for everyone."

THE CLOTHES LINE

A tale from the Middle East

IN A POOR corner of old Jerusalem was a jumble of dwellings huddled around a courtyard. Perhaps the houses had once been separate, but over the generations people had built and built: rooms to the side and rooms to the back and even rooms on top. The houses had been built so high that the courtyard only caught the earliest rays of morning sunshine.

Knowing this, one woman got up early to wash the household bedding. She fetched some water and dipped the sheets. She soaped them and squeezed them and sluiced them clean. Then she took the clean sheets and hung them in the courtyard to dry.

Another woman saw the sheets and only then she remembered.

"It's a fine day, and if I work quickly, I can do my washing and hang it to dry in the last of the early morning sunshine."

She fetched some water and dipped the sheets. She soaped them and squeezed them and sluiced them clean. Then she took the clean sheets out to the courtyard to dry.

"What a nuisance," she said when she saw her neighbour's sheets billowing in the breeze. "But they're almost dry, and anyway it's my turn to have the line."

She pulled down the damp sheets and left them in a heap on the ground. Then she pegged out her own sheets and left them to dry, even though the last of the morning sunshine was slipping away.

The first woman returned just moments later to find her sheets lying on the ground, streaked with dust.

"Oh dear!" she grumbled. "This is too bad."

She gathered the washing up and took it home. Then she fetched more water and dipped the soiled sheets. She soaped them and squeezed them and sluiced them clean. Then she left them in a basket until the clothes line might be free.

It was late afternoon when the second woman came to collect her sheets. She folded each one in half and half and half again. She piled them in her basket and went home singing.

The first woman sighed. The sun had disappeared behind the rooftops and there would be no point hanging out her sheets until the morning. Well, she would have to tell her family that they must make do with blankets that night.

She was explaining the problem as they were gathering for the evening meal when someone came banging on the door.

"I need your help," said the second woman. "My husband's family have come unexpectedly to stay. Do you have any clean sheets to lend me?"

"I do have clean sheets," said the first woman. "But sadly they are not yet dry."

AXE PORRIDGE

A tale from Russia

THE SOLDIER SAT on a stone by the edge of a village and sighed. He had been given leave to go home, but without money he had no choice but to walk there. Now the sun had set and drained the landscape of colour. He would have to seek lodgings for the night.

He went to the nearest house and knocked on the door.

An old woman came and opened it a crack. She eyed the visitor warily.

The soldier explained who he was and why he had come. "I would be so grateful just to sleep under a roof for the night," he said. "The air is already cold and a hard frost threatens."

"Come in," said the old woman somewhat grudgingly.

She showed the man where he should leave his boots and then gestured for him to sit down on a wooden seat near the fire.

"Thank you," said the soldier. "You are so kind."

The woman threw a log on the fire and returned to her darning. The log fizzed and crackled in the fire. The soldier dozed a little. Then he opened his eyes and began to look around him.

The woman really did have very little. And although he was very grateful that she had allowed him to stay, he was beginning to feel extremely hungry.

"I was wondering," he said hesitantly, "if you might be able to give me something to eat."

The old woman jabbed her needle into her work and looked up, her eyes both angry and sad. "I haven't eaten myself since yesterday," she said. "I don't know how I'll scrape my next meal together."

"Ah," said the soldier. "Times are hard for all of us."

As they sat together in silence, the man noticed an axe head lying in the corner.

"Is that something I could use?" he asked the old woman. "I think it would make excellent axe porridge."

"Axe porridge!" exclaimed the old woman.

"An old military recipe," said the soldier. "Can you show me where to fetch water? I'll go and clean the axe and fill the cooking pot."

The old woman pointed the soldier to a well further down the road. He returned, whistling.

"So here is the cooking pot with the axe inside and a quantity of water.

"Now I'll set it over the fire and bring it to the boil."

The woman watched as the soldier fetched a spoon and began to stir the pot. Soon steam began to rise and the water began to bubble and roll.

"It's a little thinner than I hoped," said the soldier. "It's a pity you don't have any buckwheat."

"Oh, I've got some buckwheat," said the woman. She brought a crock from the cupboard and emptied the contents into the pot.

"Ooh," said the soldier, stirring hard. "That's coming along nicely."

He lifted the spoon to take the merest taste.

"Good," he said. "It is nicer with salt, but not to worry."

"Oh, there's always a bit of salt in the shaker," said the woman,

and she brought it to the soldier, who shook it in with the style of a master chef.

"This is excellent," said the soldier. "The tsar himself eats no better than this, apart from the luxury of butter."

"Oh," said the old woman, "I was forgetting. There's some in the pantry."

She brought out half a pat of butter. "Is this enough?" she asked anxiously.

"More than enough," said the soldier. "Now I just stir it in... then I take out the axe head... and it's done."

"It's very, very good," said the old woman as she and the soldier ate together. "Whoever would have thought you could get such a good meal with just an axe."

The soldier smiled as he ladled some more into her bowl.

THE PRICE OF EGGS

A tale from the Middle East

A WEALTHY KING WAS making a long journey. One morning he set out as soon as the sun rose, for he knew that it was many miles to the next town.

His guide chose the shortest route he knew, away from the main highway and along the rough tracks that threaded their way through the mountains.

The day wore on, and when the king came to a small village and saw an inn, he realized how very hungry he felt.

"We will stop here for something to eat," he told his guide. "Ask the innkeeper what he can serve us."

The guide went to enquire and returned with the news that the man could cook a plate of eggs for the king.

The innkeeper looked overawed as the king stepped into the dark interior and seated himself on a bench at the table. The regular customers – farmers and drovers – edged into the shadows and spoke in whispers.

The king listened. From inside the kitchen the innkeeper's wife sounded frantic as she gave instructions to her husband.

"Make sure you don't let any eggshell fall into the bowl.

"Here – let me stir. We want a dish for a king, not a commoner.

"Not that bowl, it's chipped… Oh, let me look for one."

After much commotion, the innkeeper burst back into the room, bearing a rough (but unchipped) pottery bowl. Within it were eggs, beautifully cooked with snipped herbs and speckled with pepper.

"Your Majesty," he said as, with a flourish, he laid the dish before the king.

The king ate. It was just the meal he had hoped for.

"Delicious," he said as he wiped his mouth. "Now, how much do I owe you?"

"A hundred gold coins," said the innkeeper.

"A HUNDRED!" said the king. "Eggs must be expensive here in these mountains. Are they scarce?"

"Oh no, not at all," said the innkeeper. "But kings are very rarely seen."

THE WISE MAN AND THE THIEF

A tale from the Far East

THERE WAS ONCE a wise man who had chosen to live a quiet and simple life. He had made his home not on a tiny plot, but on one that others had rejected. It stood on thin and stony soil, a little way out of town and somewhat further from the well than was convenient.

Patiently he had worked to make his garden flourish, and when he took his produce to market, people were eager to buy.

"His are the tastiest vegetables," everyone agreed. "It must be the careful way he manages the soil and the thoughtful way he waters it just the right amount."

For such good food, they were willing to pay good prices.

The money that could made from a small vegetable garden did not amount to a great deal, but because the wise man did not spend on luxuries, he had enough for all his needs.

"And maybe some more besides," thought an idle young man who had come sneaking around the market that day.

That evening, when the wise man was hoeing the weeds in his garden, the young man sprung upon him, brandishing a sword.

"Hand me your money," he demanded with a snarl, "or you'll be sorry."

The wise man looked up calmly. "My money," he replied, "is in the jar beside my bed. Do go and fetch it."

The thief dashed inside and found the jar. There were fewer

coins than he was hoping, but he scooped them greedily into his sack.

He was just tying the top shut when the wise man appeared in the doorway.

"I meant to ask," he said, "if you would leave me one silver coin. I need it tomorrow to pay the rent on my home."

The thief was astonished. No one had ever stopped him in the middle of a robbery before. He reached for a silver coin and tossed it at the man before dashing past him.

"You are forgetting," called the wise man, "to say thank you. It's important to be polite."

The thief felt a chill of fear. How could an old fool have him so unnerved? He glanced back.

"Thanks," he mumbled, and with that, he dashed away.

A few days later, the town clerk came to visit the old man. With him came armed men who had the thief under arrest.

"We have reason to believe," said the clerk, "that this man has robbed you. He has certainly robbed others, and we are trying to establish the extent of his depravity."

The wise man looked up and leaned thoughtfully on his spade.

Then he smiled at the town clerk.

"This man didn't rob me," he said. "I gave him some money not so long ago, and he thanked me for it."

"Did he?" said the town clerk. "Oh. That changes things somewhat. Thank you." Even so, he wore a puzzled expression as he gestured for his party to follow him away.

The young man was tried for his wrongdoing, but because of what the wise man had said, did not receive too severe a punishment.

When he was released from prison, he came and found the wise man.

"I've come to thank you properly," he said. "And I was just wondering… I need an honest trade and was hoping you might teach me about gardening."

Why the Wasp Can't Make Honey

A tale from Jamaica

ALL THE CLEVER things that creatures can do – don't think they all come naturally! Long ago, all the animals had to go to school. The birds had to learn flying, singing, and nest building. The hens had to learn a complete vocabulary of clucking, as well as egg laying and chick rearing. The lizards had to learn basking and scuttling, and the chameleons had to stay for extra lessons to learn colour changing and tail curling. As for the cows, they had to learn how to chew the grass slowly to make good milk. A few of the cows also did an optional course in weather forecasting, but it was not a huge success.

The insects had to go to school as well. The old mongoose who taught them soon found that insects were all very different. Some could dart from one thing to another and grasped ideas in a flash. Others were slow and bumbling.

Not that the brightest pupils always learn the best. The wasp was very clever, but he was also very naughty. He was forever buzzing around, annoying the other pupils, and he did not follow the rules about when to sting and when to let things go.

The bee was among the bumblers. He didn't work very fast, but he never stopped trying.

"Such a contrast with the wasp," the old mongoose told the other teachers. "I've just finished the class on nest building. The wasp made something brilliant out of paper and it took almost no time. The bee was very careful but oh, so slow. And just how many honeycombs does a nest need? Once the bee gets the idea, he just keeps going.

"I can hardly bear to go back to teach honey making."

Even so, she was a dedicated teacher and she set about her task. She told the wasp and the bee what kind of flowers were best for nectar. She showed them how to sip it and take it to the nest.

"Urghh, the flowers are all dusty with pollen," complained the wasp. "I'd rather find an easier way to get food."

He was so naughty that when it was time for the class to put into practice what they had learned, he slipped away from school: he went and made a nuisance of himself in the apple orchard.

The bee went slowly from flower to flower, dipping its tongue for the nectar and moving on. From time to time it flew back to the nest to store what it had collected in the honeycombs it had built.

When the time came to assess the task, the bee got the best mark of all. He went to do a vocational course in honey making, and when he grew up, he set up his own honey business. Everyone wanted to buy bee honey.

As for the wasp… he never learned to make honey. When he realized how he'd missed out on a huge opportunity, he developed a severe grudge. But he didn't reform. Oh no. He still flies around breaking the rules about stinging and making a nuisance of himself in the apple orchard.

THE LION AND THE HARE

A tale from Africa

THE ANIMALS HAD made their way secretly and silently across the plain. In the shade of a cluster of thornbushes, they gazed at one another solemnly.

Buffalo was the first to speak.

"Lion has brought misery to our land," he said. "He is fierce and brave, and for that reason, he has become our king; but now he rules us as a tyrant, chasing and killing for no reason other than to show his strength."

"And his speed," added Gazelle.

"And his cunning," agreed Fox.

"And his teeth and his claws," clucked Quail, and the reminder set the entire flock of quails clucking and flapping.

"Sshhh," said Hare. "What's the point of a secret meeting if you make a noise like that?"

The birds fell silent. All the animals bowed their heads in thought. A few butterflies flitted above the grasses, but they were not part of the meeting and their carefree dancing did nothing to cheer anyone.

"I cannot think of any remedy," continued Buffalo, "other than to make an agreement with Lion. Every day, we will draw lots. In this way, we will choose each day who is to feed Lion."

The quails started squawking again.

"Sshhh," said Hare.

"But we know what 'feeding' means," said Quail. "It doesn't mean taking Lion a meal. It means BEING the meal."

"Do you have a better idea?" asked Buffalo. None of the animals replied. Not even Hare.

There was a moment of whispering and a somewhat longer moment when a few tears were shed, but in the end the plan was agreed.

The animals went to Lion and pleaded with him to accept the bargain.

"You are our king," announced Buffalo humbly. "It is right that we should serve you in this way."

"I think it's a rather good idea," said Lion. He yawned and stretched. Hmmm. He was thinking it was really quite splendid that he was being accorded such respect; how delightful it would be to laze in the sunshine, waiting for his meal to arrive... and how easily he could break his side of the bargain if he grew bored with it.

For some time, the plan worked. The grief of the families who watched a loved one make the final walk to Lion seemed a lesser misery than the daily fear that once haunted every family, day and night.

Now Hare had never thought the idea was a good one. He just couldn't think of a different one. Then came the day when lots were drawn and he was chosen to go to Lion. As is often the case, panic sharpens the wits.

As the animals gathered to say their last goodbyes, Hare waved his paw to silence them.

"Don't get all sentimental," he said, "and above all, don't say ridiculously nice things about me that you don't mean. You're going to have to stand by whatever you say. I'm coming back."

"Hare," said Buffalo sternly, "you do understand that you are Lion's next meal?"

The quails clucked and fluttered in alarm. "Don't say it so brutally," they complained.

"Let him say it," said Hare. "The facts are brutal. We are ruled by a tyrant. It's time to end the arrangement. Now, if you don't mind, I must be off."

He bounded away, leaving his friends looking gloomy.

Did he hurry to Lion? No, he did not.

Hare bounded off and hid in the long grass. He watched the butterflies dancing. They made him smile.

He watched the sun sink low and melt into an orange sunset.

He watched the first star shine out in the darkening twilight.

Then he bounded over to Lion and arrived gasping for breath.

"RRRAARGGH! I'm so hungry," snarled Lion.

"I know, I know," said Hare. "I'm late, and what's worse is that there's only me."

"That's right, there's only you to blame for why I'm so hungry I could EAT A BUFFALO!" roared Lion.

"I'm so, so sorry," wailed Hare. "But listen: a dreadful thing happened. I, being small, was chosen alongside my bigger brother to round out your meal. And we were both on our way when ANOTHER lion came and snatched my bigger brother…"

"Another lion?" Lion narrowed his eyes. "Are you saying there is another lion who has come into my territory?"

Hare nodded frantically. "That's right," he said. "Another lion is challenging you – he has already taken food that was practically in your mouth.

RRRAARGGHHHHHH!

Lion gave the most terrifying roar. "Where can I find him?" he demanded to know.

"I think I can show you," said Hare, "if you could postpone your meal for long enough."

"Take me to my ENEMY!" roared Lion, and Hare nodded and nodded.

"Follow," he said.

Hare bounded and skipped ahead of Lion in the moonlight,

always taking care to stay just that extra bound ahead in case Lion changed his mind. He led Lion across the plain and through a thicket of trees.

"There," he said, pointing to a ring of stones. "I saw him in there. If you go near enough, you'll see him; but don't go into his lair. You'd be better waiting here in the shadows, so you can spring a surprise attack."

"Wait?" said Lion. "I'm too hungry to wait. That interloper won't live a moment after I've set eyes on him."

"Then come," said Hare. "Come quietly. Shh."

The two animals crept over to the ring of stones. Hare went first and nodded. "Come and see," he mouthed.

Lion crouched low and looked.

In a deep den was the other lion and the other hare.

He crouched and sprang.

SPLASH

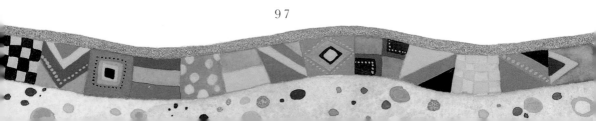

Afterwards, Hare loved telling the story of how Lion had sprung at his own reflection. He had tumbled over the stones into a deep, deep pool from which he had never surfaced.

"Well done," said Buffalo. "Brave and good Hare."

"But your brother," said the quails. "What happened to him?"

THE BELL OF ATRI

A tale from Italy

LONG AGO IN Italy lived a king who was famous for his wisdom. King Giovanni ruled the city of Atri, and kings and emperors from far and wide would often ask his advice.

It was for such a reason that he once had to go on long journey. He knew he would be away for some time, and before he left, he ordered a bell tower to be built right in the centre of the market square. He had a great bell made to hang in the tower, with a long rope that dangled almost to the ground.

He gathered the people in the square.

"In my kingdom," he said, "no one's cries for justice should go unheard. If anyone has a grievance that they cannot settle without help, they should ring this bell.

"I have commanded the judges to go and speak with whoever asks for justice in this way, and they will look into the matter and pursue it until it is resolved."

The plan worked very well. In fact, for the first year the judges were very busy as more and more people dared to come and ring the bell of justice.

No longer did the people who came to market have to put up with stallholders who used false weights. No longer did apprentices have to suffer miserable living conditions. No longer did craftspeople have to accept being paid by the piece rather than by the hour, forcing them to work late into the night even to scrape a living.

Neither did the judges favour one kind of person more than another. Indeed, whenever a child rang the bell, the judges came even more quickly to see what was the problem, even if it turned out to be little more than a playtime quarrel.

As for anyone who might be tempted to cheat or bully or steal… they quickly came to fear the sound of the bell. For them, its golden chime might well be followed by the clang of a prison gate. It seemed that everyone understood that it was right to be fair and honest and kind.

Time went by. The hemp bellrope began to fray. It froze in the winter wet and frittered away in the summer heat. But no one noticed how worn it had become, for no one needed to use it.

One day, a herald rode into the marketplace. "The king is at the city gate," he announced. "He wants to see how his kingdom has fared while he has been away, and there is no time to put up any pretence."

Even so, in the few minutes before he would surely arrive, everyone strove to make everything look its best. Stallholders tidied their produce into heaps, the street minstrels retuned their instruments, children rushed to gather up chickens and cats, and the judges went to the bell tower.

"Oh no!" they gasped. "We have neglected to keep the bell in working order. What can we do?"

"I've got an idea," said a young farmer's lad. He dashed to his cart and came back with an armful of long straw. "I can weave this in and tie it," he said, "and it will look almost as good as a proper rope…"

"… which we can say is being made as part of ongoing maintenance," agreed the judges.

When the king arrived in the marketplace, everything was as ready as it could be.

"I am pleased," said King Giovanni as he walked around. "I am glad to see that the instructions I left with you have been followed, and it seems that everyone is prospering."

He went into the city hall to meet with his senior advisers and his judges.

The sun went past its highest point. The market square emptied as people retreated into the shade for the hottest part of the day. In the city hall, those meeting with the king were now gathered around a feast.

kerlang kerlang kerlang

Into the hot and lazy afternoon came the old clamour for justice. The king and his judges hurried to see what was the matter.

There was a poor horse, lame and bony, chewing desperately on the straw that had been used to fix the bell rope.

"Who has neglected this poor creature?" the king demanded to know.

"We've never seen it before," the judges insisted. "Has it just wandered in?"

A boy stepped forward. "Don't you recognize it?" he said. "It's an old warhorse. The soldier who lives just outside the town has no use for it anymore, so he just leaves him in a tiny paddock."

The king turned to face the judges and the judges looked shocked.

"We really had no idea about this," they said.

"Now we do know," said King Giovanni, "and we must put things right at once. Even the animals deserve to be treated fairly."

So it was done. The horse was given good pasture, a new rope was hung, and every new year, a child was invited to reach up and ring the bell to prove that justice was in reach of everyone.

ABELARD AND THE THREE GIFTS

A folk tale from France

WHEN ABELARD was young, he lived in a little house with his mother and his father. They provided him with everything he needed.

When he was still just a boy, both his parents died and Abelard was left an orphan.

However, he was not entirely alone, for when he was born, his mother and father had chosen for him three godparents who lived in another country. When these three heard the sad news, they each came in turn to offer what help they could.

The first one arrived with tears in her eyes. "What a tragedy," she wept. "I have come to take care of you until you are older.

Look, I have brought you a quilt that is soft and deep. You can wrap yourself in its warmth and protect yourself from the cruel and bitter world."

Abelard took the quilt gladly. The dark days of mourning were eased a little by the soft comfort of the quilt, and Abelard's godmother did all she could to protect him from any more sorrow and harm.

When Abelard was almost grown up, the second of his godparents came to visit. This godfather came striding up the path to the house, calling out his greeting. He knocked firmly on the door.

"Come, Abelard," he said. "We all have to make our way in the world some time. You are young and strong, and I can help you find work on the farms and in the workshops. In time you will have to choose a trade for yourself and earn your own living."

Then his godfather opened the pack he was carrying and took out a pair of stout leather boots. "Here," he said. "You will need these as a working man."

The boots fitted well, and Abelard did as his godfather instructed him.

He learned how to care for the sheep on the hills and how to steer the plough through the fields in the valley. He learned how to sow seed and reap the harvest.

He learned how to fell trees and saw them into planks, and how to fashion the wood into the everyday things that people needed.

He learned how to set the sails of the windmill to grind the grain to make flour.

After seven years, he said to his godfather, "I am a grown man now, and you have helped me to learn so many things. I am ready to go to work for my fortune in a new land."

His godfather readily agreed, and together they made the necessary preparations.

At last, Abelard was ready to set off for the port from which he would sail. He packed his quilt and was cheered to remember the love he had received as a child.

He laced his boots and smiled to think that he had the skill and strength he needed to succeed at whatever task he undertook.

But as he took one final look at the valley where he had grown up, he felt lost. How would he make his way across the trackless seas and into a little-known land?

It was then that the third of his godparents arrived to walk with him.

This godparent was an old man, grey-haired and wrinkled. Yet Abelard saw at once that he had eyes of clearest blue that danced and twinkled.

"You are about to begin a great journey," he explained to Abelard, "and it will not be long before I shall make my journey into the next. But before we part, accept my gift."

He pulled from his pocket a simple wooden flute and deftly played a merry melody. "Keep this with you always and learn to play your own tunes," he said. "Sometimes your heart will be heavy and sometimes your body will be weary, but this music will always help your spirit to dance."

THE NIGHTINGALE

Based on a tale by Hans Christian Andersen

LONG AGO THERE lived in China an emperor whose city was the most splendid in the world. The palace itself was made of porcelain, crafted with the utmost skill and painted with delicacy and grace. Even so, it was as nothing compared with the gardens.

The plants that bloomed there had been brought as tributes from far and wide. They were arranged in elegant beds so that their colours and their shapes formed intricate patterns that changed with the seasons.

Beyond the palace grounds, the land reached down through a wood of tall, dark trees and on to the ocean sea where ships with bright sails fluttered to and fro.

There on the shore lived a fisherman.

"Though I am poor, I have a greater treasure than the emperor," he used to say to himself. "For my home is near where a nightingale nests, and the bird's song brings me joy through the darkness."

It so happened that many people came on long journeys across the world to see the imperial city and its wonders. They were allowed along a path that ran along the edge of the palace gardens, next to the wood, and those who were there in the evening would sometimes hear the nightingale.

"What an enchanting melody," they agreed. "Everything about our visit has been a delight, but the song of the nightingale is the best of all."

Those visitors who were poets wrote about the song, and the poems appeared in books, and the books were read all around the world – and some were brought to the emperor.

"What is this?" he said to his courtiers. "People are saying that the song of the nightingale is the best thing in my empire… and yet I have never heard it."

Servants were sent hurrying to try to find the bird, but without success. The chief courtier was anxious about what to do next to meet the emperor's request.

"I can help," said a little girl, who was just a scullery maid. "I hear the nightingale when I walk through the woods to my home. I can show you where it nests."

That evening she led him through the shadows of the trees

to the spot she knew so well. "There is the nightingale," she said. She pointed to a pale, grey-brown bird, almost hidden among the leaves.

"Oh," said the chief courtier. "It is quite shabby to look at. Is its song really so wonderful?"

The little bird opened its beak, and out tumbled a trill of notes – pure, clear, and joyful.

The chief courtier clapped his hands and bowed to the little bird. "That is quite wonderful," he said. "Will you come and sing for the emperor?"

"My song sounds best here in the wood," replied the nightingale, "but it will be my pleasure to bring joy into the palace, if that is what the emperor wishes."

The very next day the nightingale came and sang, and the emperor was as delighted as all the others who had heard the song.

"The bird must stay in the palace," declared the emperor. "It will have a fine golden cage. Twice a day and once at night it will be taken out into the gardens. But it must be kept safe."

The nightingale had little choice. Yet it drooped within its cage and scarcely fluttered when it went into the gardens, for all the time it was held by a silken cord attached to its leg. Its only joy was to see how the emperor and his courtiers smiled whenever it sang its song.

One day, a package was delivered to the palace. Inside was a note:

"The emperor of China's nightingale is poor compared to this nightingale sent as a gift from the emperor of Japan."

The servants delved among the paper packaging and pulled out an exquisite cage. Inside was a bird in the shape of a nightingale – but ornamented with diamonds, rubies, and sapphires. As soon as the bird was wound up, it trilled a perfect little song and bobbed up and down.

"Perfect," said the emperor. "Now that woodland bird can stop its sulking and go back and live in the wood. This masterpiece will stay in the palace."

So the jewelled mechanical bird trilled its songs. Each one was perfect. Night after night it sang without complaining; and of course, there was no need to take it out to the gardens.

One evening, in the midst of a glittering glissando of notes, the jewelled bird stopped. The emperor sent for a watchmaker to see if it could be repaired; but after painstaking work, he had to declare that its inner workings were worn and that there was very little hope it would sing again.

Time passed, and the emperor became unwell. He lay on his couch fretting: about all the things he had done in his life and those that could not be changed; about the little time that was left him to choose the things that were good and worthwhile.

His eyes fell on the jewelled bird. "Why don't you sing again!" he cried. "Oh, I feel so alone."

Just then the smell of roses clambering outside his window

wafted in. Then on the breeze came a wonderful waterfall of notes.

"My woodland nightingale!" exclaimed the emperor. "I was wrong to send you away. You are kind to return."

The nightingale hopped onto the windowsill.

"You did right in letting me go," said the bird. "I sing to bring joy to everyone: the fisherman and the kitchen maid, the pilgrim and the poet. If you are content to listen in their company, I will sing for you as well."

THE MOST PRECIOUS GIFT

A tale from the Near East

FROM THE DECK of the great sailing ship, the merchants looked anxiously down. The last of the cargo was being brought on board. Each of them was anxious to see that their crates and chests had been loaded. Were their servants checking carefully enough? Were the porters being gentle with their precious goods? Were any light-fingered scoundrels roaming by the dock, trying to pilfer something for themselves?

As the last of the porters scurried off down the gangplank and the sailors began to untie the ropes, the merchants breathed a sigh of relief and began to talk among themselves.

"I hear the price of gold is up again. But will that affect sales of gold jewellery?"

"Silver is much less sought after. Except for tableware, of course, and that is all the fashion among the very wealthy."

"There has been much banditry on the silk road. Fortunately my suppliers are, shall we say, properly informed about the best way to avoid trouble from the gangs of robbers."

As they talked, they began to notice one man on deck who was simply admiring the way the wind filled the sails of the ship as it left the shelter of the coast for the open sea.

"Do you know that man?"

"Has he come this route before?"

"What goods does he deal in?"

As they gathered below deck for supper, they began to ask, but the stranger seemed not to want to talk business.

"The reason for my voyage is to give a gift," he said.

"It must be expensive that you undertake so long a voyage to deliver it," exclaimed his questioner.

"Well, it is precious," was all the stranger would say.

Wondering what it might be became a popular topic of conversation. After all, the man was no one's rival in business; and he was pleasant to be with – as eager to listen as to tell stories, and with a nice turn of phrase.

After several days out at sea, the ship turned closer to the coast of the country to which they were going. However, the weather had turned colder. A strong breeze drove in squalls. As night fell the sea began to rise and fall. Then the swelling waves began to lash and crash over the side.

"Everyone get on deck!" cried the captain. "We're going to try and run the boat onto the beach. If the boat breaks up, swim for your lives!"

For what seemed like hours the boat lurched forward toward land, only to be sucked back. People from the nearby villages came to the beach and watched, wanting so much to help yet powerless against the sea. Just as dawn was breaking, the boat keeled over and everyone on board was pitched into the water.

Desperately everyone made for the beach – some swimming, some others clinging desperately onto bits of wreckage, kicking and screaming.

Somehow everyone was finally hauled from the water. The boat rasped against the pebbles as it was dragged back out to sea. It hit a reef and broke up. The cargo was lost.

The villagers welcomed those who had been shipwrecked and helped them travel the final few miles to the port to which they had been sailing.

There the merchants went to the harbour and began begging for somewhere to stay and food to eat.

The stranger with the gift did not join them. He went to the marketplace and began to speak.

"I am a scholar," he explained. "I have studied law – not as a judge but as one who seeks to guide people to do what is good and right."

A large crowd gathered. The man told good stories and had a nice turn of phrase. He listened to questions and answered them wisely. He was invited to speak at the local university. A fee was arranged. Grateful students offered hospitality and also brought gifts. He made good friends, both among the common people and those who were wealthy and influential.

When a ship arrived that would enable everyone to return to their home port, only the stranger who had studied law had enough to pay his way.

He spoke to the townspeople on behalf of the merchants. "Please lend them what they need in order to return home. When they have rebuilt their trade, they will return to repay you."

So it was agreed. As the merchants stood on deck watching the bustle beside the dock, they thought sorrowfully of the day they had set sail and how much they had lost since then.

They turned to the scholar. "Are you sad that you were not able

to deliver your gift to the person for whom it was intended?"

"But I did deliver it!" said the teacher. "The most precious gift of all is to help people understand what is good and right."

THE BOATMAN

A world story

A MAN WHO WAS famous for his learning set out for a distant town. As he journeyed, he came to a river. The recent rains had made it burst its banks, and now it spread across the valley nearly half a mile wide.

The scholar hurried over to a boatman who was sitting on a log near where the river met the road. His rickety wooden boat was pulled up on the grass.

"Can you take me across?" he asked anxiously. "I am invited as the guest speaker at a great university and I do not want to be late."

The boatman gazed out across the water.

"It's risky," he said. "The heavy rain is flooding down from the

mountains, and who knows what it's brought with it."

The man scanned the expanse of water. "I can't see anything," he said. "Please take me across."

The boatman agreed and paddled the man out into the river. It was slow going, as the current was so strong. The boatman angled his craft skilfully and rowed strongly.

His passenger grew bored. "I'm a philosopher," he told the man. "Have you read any philosophy?"

The boatman shook his head.

"It's very interesting," said the man eagerly. "In fact, I could let you have a book I wrote that would be the perfect introduction to the subject."

"Thank you, but I've got no use for it," said the boatman. "I never learned to read."

"Oh dear!" exclaimed the scholar. "You've wasted half your life!"

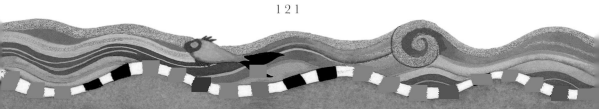

The boatman shrugged and pulled on the oars. The boat was now halfway across the water, where the main course of the river ran.

thwack

From nowhere, a half-submerged log floating on the flood struck the boat hard, nearly upsetting it.

The man tutted to himself as he settled back in his seat. He lifted his cloak out of the water that had somehow spilled into the bottom of the boat. He was looking forward to getting back onto land.

From behind him the boatman spoke.

"Have you ever learned to swim?" he asked.

"No, I haven't," snapped the scholar.

"That's a shame," said the boatman. "You've wasted all your life. I'm afraid the boat is sinking."

THE RIVER THAT MOVED

A tale from Asia Minor

FOR AS LONG as anyone could remember, the people had lived by the river.

It provided everything. It gave water for drinking, water for washing, and water to irrigate the crops.

It teemed with fish that were good for eating.

It carried the people's boats down to the great cities by the sea, and yet its gentle current always allowed them to return upstream to their home.

Its banks and its shallows were lovely places to play.

All of the people's traditions – their stories, their songs, and their beliefs – had something to do with the river. Each year they held a great festival in celebration of it, with joyful parties held

on brightly lit boats that danced on the moonlit ripples.

"Hooray for our river!" cried the children. "May it flow for ever."

One year, however, the river was a little lower than everyone had hoped.

"Each season is different," the old people agreed. "The last months have seen little rain, but our river will never fail."

But the river continued to fall.

"Unless the flow returns to normal, we will have to be careful how much water we use for our crops," said the men.

"And the water we collect is more bitter than it was and not so clean," complained the women.

"And the river is not such a nice place to play," complained the children.

124

That year, the festival was not a success. There was so little water that the decorated boats were scarcely floating. The cries of "hooray" were faint and half-hearted.

A month later, the riverbed was almost dry. The children who gathered by the riverbank grew sulky.

"What can we do now?" they asked one another.

Then a girl spoke. "I know," she said. "Let's go and find the river!"

All the children jumped to their feet. "Yes, let's go," they said. And they raced off to tell their families of the great plan.

"But you have no idea what kind of journey you face," warned their parents. "Who can tell what has happened? You may walk and walk, and all for nothing."

"If the river is still flowing, then it will flow here," grumbled the grandparents. "Here is where it belongs. Our stories say so. Our songs say so. We say so too."

"But at least we can go and look," argued the children. "It's worth a try."

At last it was agreed, and a great party of young people set off to find the river that gave them life.

The way was long and hard: up the mountain tracks and into the blue horizon.

After many days' marching, they crossed a mountain pass, and what they saw dazzled their eyes: a waterfall so high, so pure, so beautiful it seemed it must be tumbling from the sky.

"Look!" they cried. "There is the river! A fall of rock has made it change course, but now it is tumbling into another valley, and a new land is green with meadows and bright with flowers."

Joyfully they returned home.

"Good news," they said. "The river is flowing in a new direction. We can move and make for ourselves a new home."

"But here is your home – and our home too," said the parents.

"And this is where our people's homes have always been and must always be," said the old people.

"But we cannot live here without the river," said the girl who had first had the idea of going to find it. She looked around. All the people had gathered to hear of their journey of discovery, but now they were not wanting to listen to what they heard.

"We cannot stay here," she said again. "We must be bold enough to follow the river, for that is the source of everything."

Her words fell into an anxious silence. The people looked at her, fearful and hostile.

Then her own grandmother stood up, straightening herself as she gripped the stick she used for walking.

"I shall always love this place and the traditions of the old days," she announced. "But if the river has moved, then I will go to find it in the place where it is.

"That place will be my new home, and there we will celebrate again."